La Constitución de los EE.UU./
The U.S. Constitution

por/by Kathy Allen

Traducción/Translation: Dr. Martín Luis Guzmán Ferrer

Editor Consultor/Consulting Editor: Dra. Gail Saunders-Smith

Consultor/Consultant: Philip Bigler
Director, The James Madison Center
Harrisonburg, Virginia

Capstone
press

Mankato, Minnesota

Pebble Plus is published by Capstone Press,
151 Good Counsel Drive, P.O. Box 669, Mankato, Minnesota 56002.
www.capstonepress.com

1 2 3 4 5 6 13 12 11 10 09 08

Library of Congress Cataloging-in-Publication Data
Allen, Kathy.
  [U.S. Constitution. Spanish & English]
  La Constitución de los EE.UU. / por Kathy Allen = The U.S. Constitution / by Kathy Allen.
  p. cm. — (Pebble plus)
  Includes index.
  ISBN-13: 978-1-4296-0046-0 (hardcover)
  ISBN-10: 1-4296-0046-2 (hardcover)
  1. United States. Constitution — Juvenile literature. 2. Constitutional history — United States — Juvenile
literature. I. Title. II. Title: U.S. Constitution.
E303.A4418 2008
320.973 — dc22   2007031358

Summary: Simple text and photographs introduce the U.S. Constitution, its history, and significance — in both
    English and Spanish.

Editorial Credits
Martha E. H. Rustad, editor; Katy Kudela, bilingual editor; Eida del Risco, Spanish copy editor; Linda Clavel,
    designer; Deirdre Barton, photo researcher/photo editor

Photo Credits
Art Resource, NY/Christy Howard Chander, 12–13
Corbis/Francis G. Mayer, 6–7, 11 (left); Geoffrey Clements, 11 (right); Ariel Skelley, 20–21
Getty Images Inc./Todd Gipstein, cover
North Wind Picture Archives, 8–9
Photodisc, 1 (right); 15 (middle), 17
Shutterstock/Brandon Seidel, 1 (left); Scott Rothstein, 4–5; Manoj Valappil, 15 (left); bluestocking, 15 (right);
    Jason Maehl, 18–19

Note to Parents and Teachers

This book supports national standards related to power, authority, and governance. This book describes and illustrates la Constitución de los EE.UU./the U.S. Constitution in both English and Spanish. The images support early readers in understanding the text. The repetition of words and phrases helps early readers learn new words. This book also introduces early readers to subject-specific vocabulary words, which are defined in the Glossary section. Early readers may need assistance to read some words and to use the Table of Contents, Glossary, Internet Sites, and Index sections of the book.

Table of Contents

Tabla de contenidos

What Is the Constitution?

The Constitution is a document.

It is the basic law of

the United States.

¿Qué es la Constitución?

La Constitución es un documento.

Es la ley fundamental de

los Estados Unidos.

Making the U.S. Constitution

The United States was created

after the Revolutionary War.

The country needed a

new government.

Cómo se hizo la Constitución de los EE.UU.

Estados Unidos se creó después

de la Guerra de Independencia.

El país necesitaba un

gobierno nuevo.

In 1787, the country's
leaders met. They worked
all summer long to write
the Constitution.

En 1787, los líderes del país
se reunieron. Trabajaron durante
todo el verano para escribir
la Constitución.

George Washington led the meetings. James Madison and other leaders helped write the Constitution.

George Washington estuvo al frente de las reuniones. James Madison y los demás líderes ayudaron a escribir la Constitución.

George Washington

James Madison

A New Government

The U.S. Constitution was finished on September 17, 1787. Thirty-nine leaders signed it.

Un nuevo gobierno

La Constitución de los EE.UU. terminó de escribirse el 17 de septiembre de 1787. La firmaron treinta y nueve líderes.

The Constitution set up
the government. It gave the
government three parts. Each part
has an equal amount of power.

La Constitución estableció el
gobierno. Dividió el gobierno
en tres partes. Cada parte
tiene iguales poderes.

The Constitution/ La Constitución

President/
Presidente

Congress/
Congreso

Supreme Court/
Corte Suprema

The Bill of Rights was added
to the Constitution in 1791.
It lists the rights that the
government cannot take away.

La Carta de Derechos se añadió
a la Constitución en 1791.
Esta Carta enumera los derechos
que el gobierno debe respetar.

We the People

Bill of Rights

Congress of the United States

begun and held at the City of New York, on

Wednesday the Fourth of March, one thousand seven hundred and eighty nine.

Today, people still must
follow the Constitution.
Courts make sure that
no laws go against it.

Hoy en día, todavía la gente sigue
cumpliendo con la Constitución.
Las cortes aseguran que ninguna ley
vaya en contra de la Constitución.

Supreme Court building/
Edificio de la Corte Suprema

The Constitution keeps
our government fair.
It keeps Americans free.

La Constitución hace que tengamos
un gobierno justo. Asegura que
los estadounidenses seamos libres.

Glossary

Bill of Rights — a list of ten amendments to the Constitution that protect your right to speak freely, to practice religion, and other important rights

document — a piece of paper containing important information

equal — the same as something else in size, value, or amount

government — the people and laws that rule a town, state, country, or other area

law — a rule made by the government that must be obeyed

Revolutionary War — the war in which the 13 American colonies won their independence from Great Britain; it lasted from 1775 to 1783.

right — something the law allows people to do, such as the right to vote or the right to speak freely; the government cannot take away our rights.

Glosario

la Carta de Derechos — lista de diez enmiendas a la Constitución que protegen tus derechos a hablar con libertad, practicar tu religión y otros derechos importantes

el derecho — algo que la ley permite hacer, como el derecho al voto o el derecho a hablar con libertad; el gobierno no puede quitarnos nuestros derechos.

el documento — hoja de papel que contiene información importante

el gobierno — las personas y las leyes que rigen una ciudad, estado, país u otra zona

la Guerra de Independencia — la guerra por la cual las 13 colonias de América del Norte ganaron su independencia de Gran Bretaña; duró de 1775 a 1783.

igual — algo que tiene el mismo tamaño, valor o cantidad

la ley — una orden creada por el gobierno que debe obedecerse

Internet Sites

FactHound offers a safe, fun way to find Internet sites related to this book. All of the sites on FactHound have been researched by our staff.

Here's how:

1. Visit *www.facthound.com*

2. Choose your grade level.

3. Type in this book ID **1429600462** for age-appropriate sites. You may also browse subjects by clicking on letters, or by clicking on pictures and words.

4. Click on the **Fetch It** button.

FactHound will fetch the best sites for you!

Sitios de Internet

FactHound te brinda una manera divertida y segura de encontrar sitios de Internet relacionados con este libro. Hemos investigado todos los sitios de FactHound. Es posible que algunos sitios no estén en español.

Se hace así:

1. Visita *www.facthound.com*

2. Elige tu grado escolar.

3. Introduce este código especial **1429600462** para ver sitios apropiados a tu edad, o usa una palabra relacionada con este libro para hacer una búsqueda general.

4. Haz un clic en el botón **Fetch It**.

¡FactHound buscará los mejores sitios para ti!

Index

Índice